G. vv. VATERLAUS

DOG TAGS

BALLERINAS

G.W.Vaterlaus, Dog Tags

Published by MEDIAPLEX s.r.o.,
Holečkova 789/49, Praha 5, Czech Republic
info@mediaplex.cz

This novel is entirely a work of fiction. The names, characters and events portrayed in it are the work of the author's imagination and any resemblance to actual persons, living or dead, is entirely coincidental.

ePub: ISBN 978-80-87720-08-0
print: ISBN 978-80-87720-54-7

Preface

Claire opened the blinds and peered out the window, feeling as bleak as the gray-brown landscape of late Autumn. The laptop in front of her was forgotten as she traveled back in time to when she didn't feel so alone. As her coffee grew cold she wondered if she should have chosen a different path and If she had, would she be sitting here now, lost in thought, not caring if it were night or day, thoughts corrupted by a lonely life.

Did David ever think of her as she did of him? Was there time in his busy life of rodeos, traveling and horses to remember how good it once was? Was it even that great, had time filled the void with positive memories that had never occurred ? She doubted it. If he did, he would come home once in awhile, or call. It had been months since she had last heard his voice over the phone, and that, like the majority of calls she received since he left, had been brief and full of empty promises, like usual.

1

Admit it," she sighed to herself, pulling her curly brown hair into a make shift bun, "It's over. " There was no longer a need for her to hang on to David and the relationship they once had, it was the past she couldn't hold a candle to the rodeo rats, the glitz and glamour of a rodeo cowboys life and she knew that he had moved on, and she ultimately needed to do the same.

Getting up to top off her coffee, she heard a knock at her front door. She hurried through the kitchen and into the living room, wiping her face as she passed by the hallway mirror. Bending to the right of the door she looked out the window and noticed a massive, red Dodge truck in her driveway. No one she knew. Rural Oklahoma was pickup country, nothing new there, but no one she knew drove anything that new. Walking to the door, she glimpsed the outline of a tall man about to knock again. She opened the door revealing a tall fellow, strongly built, in faded blue jeans and a brown Carhartt jacket, dark hair cut in military fashion.

"Hello, can I help you ?" she asked , holding the door ajar with her foot.

" Hi." The handsome stranger responded in a rich deep voice to match his physique. "You wouldn't happen to have a big Golden Retriever with a red collar, would you?" He stared glassy-eyed at her , as though he would have tears running down in face in seconds.

Heart in her throat, she nodded. Images of her best friend Rusty ran through her mind as she tried to remember the last time she had seen him earlier that day. Had he gotten into someone's duck pond again, or perhaps went on one of his many walk bouts onto this strangers land?

"Ma'am, I am so sorry, everything happened so fast, He came running out of the trees and in front of my truck before I could stop. I feel so horrible, there was nothing I could do."

She cut him off, " No way, there is no way," she said moving to push past him, he caught her by the arm, and now the tears did flow as he held her gently.

" Please, just stop, you don't want to see him like this, you don't want to remember him this way. I promise you that he didn't suffer, he went fast." He muttered in a brief attempt to console her broken heart, " If you show me where you would like him buried, I will do that for you. Jesus, ma'am, it's the least I can do for you, I am so damned sorry."

Claire began to weep, and turned away. No one ever saw her cry if she could help it. She didn't know if it was a matter of pride, or if she didn't want anyone to see her in a vulnerable state. She had been alone for a long time, and had toughened up as much as single women can when they have to depend upon themselves for everything life throws at them.

"I have a small pet cemetery out back by the big oak. He should be there with the cats and birds that ended up there. There's a shovel behind the shed. It was kind of you to stop. Most wouldn't, you know."

"I am SO sorry," he said again. "Least thing I can do is see him buried with some dignity. I have a dog of my own, and a soft spot for critters. They become like your children, a part of your heart."

Wiping her eyes on her sleeve, not finding any words, she motioned him to the shed. He turned and walked around the side of the house to find the small weathered barn she kept her tools in .

Claire slumped to the floor with her back against the wall, feeling more alone now than she did ten minutes ago. Memories of Rusty flashed through her mind like a movie. Silly, rambunctious, grinning yellow dog with a heart as big as Texas. Plowing through the snow with his muzzle to the ground, splashing into the pond after ducks he couldn't catch, rolling in cow manure as though it were cologne, her one constant, the man in her life, the one that listened and never judged, he was gone...Oh, Rusty.

Things couldn't get much more depressing, she thought. Mom in a nursing home, not knowing her own daughter on bad days, David gone, her best friend Shawn Parnell deployed to Afghanistan, and now Rusty gone as well. Damn, when it rains, it pours . She sat in a miserable heap, sobbing, feeling sorry for herself. It was allowed. So much loss lately. Too much loss.

It seemed like hours, when he knocked at her door again. Standing up stiffly, she wiped her face on her now tear drenched sleeve and opened the door. When he saw her, his face crumpled and tears ran down his rugged face. She opened the door wider and motioned him inside, before gently touching his arm.

"Please don't cry, trust me, I know it was an accident, Rusty had a bad habit of focusing in on a rabbit and losing his ability to see anything else, it is not your fault, Could I offer you a cup of coffee before you go?"

He sniffled a bit, wiping his face on his right sleeve just as she had done. He had just killed her dog, and here she was, inviting him in for coffee. He looked deep into her moist gray eyes, sensing the need for a bit of human warmth, and nodded. She let him in and closed the door softly.

Looking around, he admired the rustic, Native American décor of her living room. It was warm and inviting, woven rugs, pots and throws on the couch in earth tones with vivid splashes of turquoise and burnt orange. A home suited more to a man than a woman. He wondered where her husband was, if he would mind him being here alone with her.

"Have a seat," she offered. "How do you drink your coffee?"

"Black, please."

"Coming up." She turned to the kitchen, grabbing a clean cup from the cupboard. Adding to her own cup, she took them both into the living room, handed him his, and sat down on a big leather chair covered in cowhide.

"My name is Claire, by the way," she said with a faulty smile. Her lips turned up, although she tried , but her eyes didn't match the sentiment.

" Pleased to meet you, Claire," he stood up, walked over to her chair, wiped his hands on his jeans , took her hand and shook it. "I just wish it were under different circumstances. My name is James, but my friends call me Jamie."

She nodded her head in acknowledgment, not sure what to say. He already felt bad enough, no need to say anything else. Noticing his military boots, she looked again at his haircut. High and tight. Yep, definitely a military man. She wondered what he was doing here. There were no military bases anywhere near here.

Are you in the military?" she asked, already knowing the answer, but thought it the best way to strike up a conversation.

"Yes, Ma'am. I am looking for the Parnell place. Do

you know it?"

"Yes, I sure do. Second farm down on the left. If you're looking for Shawn, I'm afraid he's in Afghanistan for the next eleven months."

Jamie, elbows on his knees, hung his head and rubbed his face with his free hand. God, she had just lost her dog, and he didn't know is she had the strength to find out that Shawn, as well, was gone, victim of an IED. Could the day get any worse?

"Have you spoken to his parents lately?" he asked quietly.

"Not since last Wednesday. They haven't been home for a few days. Haven't seen lights on down there." She replied in a questioning tone.

"Were you and Shawn close?" he asked, unsure if he should have said anything at all . Her startled eyes, like a deer in his headlights, told him she picked up on his word 'were'. He watched her shrink like a flower in early January...just sort of wilting in slow motion. She shook her head slowly in disbelief, her hand going to her cheek, but not quite landing there. Her face crumpled, and a cry flew from her soul. Claire fell forward, conscious, but gone someplace he couldn't go. He caught her before she could hit the floor, and held her in strong arms, trying to comfort, yet knowing nothing could right now. He sat on the floor and cradled her like a bereft child, rocking back and forth and smoothing her hair gently.

Claire felt her heart shatter like a broken light bulb, wondering how it could ever be whole again. Why? All of this, all of this loss, the holidays coming up, and all alone. She remembered the saying that God never gave you more than you can handle. If she even believed in God, he sure didn't know her limits very well. She wanted to find a hole, crawl into it and pull it in after her. She was vaguely aware of being held, the warmth, the solid presence of another human being holding her close.

2

Jamie's leg had gone to sleep a long time ago. Still he sat, holding her close, gently smoothing her hair back from her face. It seems she had gone to sleep, too. It made him feel strong and special that she could feel comfortable enough and trusting enough to let down her defenses and drift off. He looked down at her soft, shining brown curls, her smooth face, her strong yet feminine hand on his arm. No shirker, this gal, he reasoned. Her hands were calloused but clean, and tenderly touched his heart.

When she finally stirred, she looked up at him with sleepy eyes and smiled. Rubbing her red swollen eyes, she sat up straight, moving off his lap to sit on the floor beside him.

"Do you have someone you can call to come stay with you?" Jamie queried. "You really shouldn't be alone right now. Where is your husband?"

She looked down at her left hand while shaking her head. "I'm not married."

"A boyfriend, a good friend, anyone ?" He questioned.

"No. I thought I had a man in my life, but I guess he loves the rodeo more than me." And she started to tell him about David, the horses, and the rodeo circuit that kept him away. It was painful to admit that she was boring compared to the thrill and danger and competition of rodeo. She wasn't foolish enough to believe David was being true to her. He was a good-looking guy, and the ladies were drawn to that. He WAS a fun man, and loved his flirting.

"He's a fool," Jamie muttered. "When it comes right down to what's important, the love of a good woman will see you through the roughest of times. What will he do when he gets too old to ride bucking horses, when he can't make the grade anymore? Will he come back and expect to pick up where he left off?"

"We all make our choices and have to live with them," she sighed.

"Just because you start out on one path doesn't mean you can't backtrack and return to the one that will take you where you want to end up." Jamie looked straight into her eyes as he said "Will you take him back if he shows up?"

"I don't think so," Claire said honestly. "I'm through with being second best. I just want to be 'THE ONE', y'know? I want to matter to someone, and I can't go on not being priority in someone's life."

" Nor should you,' Jamie agreed. "You deserve to be queen to a king."

Jamie then told her a bit about himself. His parents were down in Fort Worth, ranching on land that had been in their family for generations. His parents had born and raised three rowdy boys who were all grown and on their own now. He told her of the Marines, how proud he was to belong to them and how much it meant to serve his country, even as a child he dreamed of one day becoming a Marine. She could feel his pride, seeing it shining in his eyes as he spoke of his almost four years of service. He had recently reenlisted when the girl he planned on marrying turned to another man for company, it takes a certain kind of woman to wait around for a military man, its not easy and he never faulted her for that. Even his folks didn't need him to help on the ranch, what with his youngest brother stepping into his place when he enlisted. He felt he had nothing to come back home to, his home was now wherever the Marine Corps sent him, and he was okay with that.

Jamie and Claire talked on into the evening, the sun had set drawing what little light was left into the horizon causing Jamie to turn on the lamp beside the cowhide chair. The colors and warmth of the room made Jamie feel at home, and Claire was so easy to talk to. David was a fool, Jamie thought to himself. He had a treasure and threw it away in his quest for excitement.

"Would you stay for supper?" she asked him. "I wasn't planning anything fancy, but it will be warm and filling." she finished with an uneasy smile.

"I would love to," he answered, thrilled by the invitation. He was in no hurry to leave this woman who made him feel again…feel hope and tenderness and…no, not love, he didn't know her well enough to say that. But, affection, maybe. Being around her made him feel alive and manly and needed. It was a damned good feeling.

Claire took four trout filets out of the freezer and set them in warm water to thaw, then peeled potatoes and grabbed a pack of frozen carrots, grown in her own garden, and put them in a pan with water and a bit of sea salt. Her mind raced as her hands whipped a meal she would never have made just for herself. It was grand to have someone to cook for again. Someone to sit and eat at the table with was a rare treat for her now days. This is what she had missed so very much, someone to talk with, someone who listened to what she had to say. And Jamie listened, really listened, not just waiting to turn the conversation to him. It seemed that he cared about her feelings and thoughts. David never seemed to anymore. David was becoming farther and farther from her mind as she sneaked a glance at the tall young Marine sitting in her living room.

"Is there anything I can do to help, it would be my pleasure, the least I could do, you know ?" Jamie asked.

Claire shot him a look. "Is this guy for real?" she asked herself? "No, but thanks for asking. Just make yourself comfy." He didn't hesitate, wandering about the living room, looking at pictures on the wall, the Native pots and wall hangings, the feather-decorated dream catchers. The throw rugs were colorful, the lamp adorned with two arrows, and even the drapes had an Indian motif. It was a grand room, done with taste and style. It said "Comfort" as well as being modest. None of the frilly, feminine touch that could make a man feel like a bear in a china cabinet.

"What do you do, way out here by yourself?" Jamie questioned, noticing the laptop computer on the table by the back window.

"I'm a ghost writer," she said wryly. "I write stories for other authors. Pays OK, and it lets me stay home, where I was needed when Mom was still here."

"You mean, like, you write the story, then someone else gets credit for it?" He said questioning whether or not he grasped the idea correctly.

"Yup, pretty much, sounds kind of weird when you say it like that." She said with a slanted brow.

"Why don't you write for yourself? Under your own name, I mean."

"I don't know...I started out like this, and it works for me."

Have you ever been published under your own name?" he asked.

"Nope."

"Are you currently working on anything?" he asked,

interested in what she wrote about.

"Well…I was, but today I just couldn't seem to grasp any concrete ideas that made any sense. Cabin fever, I guess," she grinned ruefully.

"How long has it been since you got out of the house, off this place?"

"I dunno, I guess a couple of weeks ago when I ran into town, I had to go to the store for something, but I cant recall what it was." She said instantly embarrassed, she had become a hermit, she never left unless she had to.

Shaking his head, he wondered if she was hiding from depression. A gal like her should have a social life, something to perk up her spirits, to get her out and about in the world. He had seen the two handsome Quarter horses out back when he was burying Rusty, and they looked fat and sassy, as though they could stand some exercise. Did she even ride them, he could tell they were well taken care of, a diet full of treats and grains, but lacking exercise.

Supper was delightful, and Jamie expressed his enjoyment. Claire blushed, but couldn't suppress a tickled smile that turned up her mouth in a very tempting way. He wondered what it would be like to kiss that mouth. But he just sat there and kept silent, knowing a kiss would be moving way too fast, considering that they had just met, and under less than ideal circumstances. He would find out, one day. She had not seen the last of him, he vowed.

They washed dishes together and talked and laughed quietly. There wasn't a morsel of food left, so there were no leftovers to deal with. As Claire put the last dish back up in the cupboard, she dried her hands and applied lotion that she kept by the sink.

"Grab your jacket," he said.

"I'm sorry?" she questioned

"Grab a warm jacket and put some boots on. I want to meet your horses. That line back mare is a sweetie, what is the gelding like?"

"He's a bit froggy, as I haven't ridden him in a few weeks."

"Would you like to go for a ride? The moon is out and it's not too cold," he suggested. Claire turned to him with a ready excuse to not go out, but then she realized that a ride with someone would be fun, and she turned to the closet to fetch her Indian print poncho, warm and wooly and just right for a night ride. Why didn't she ever do this? It was a great idea, and her mood picked up greatly. Why DIDN'T she ever do this? It used to be one of the bright spots in her days.

Walking up to the white board fence, Jamie leaned his arms on the top rail. The dun mare ambled over to sniff him, and he reached to rub her forehead. Grateful for the attention, she bobbed her head against his arm. The gelding, not wanting to miss out on anything, trotted up and gave him the eye from several paces away. Holding out his hand, the gelding decided to give him an introductory smell, then decided Jamie was friendly enough.

"Good looking animal," Jamie said to Claire as the gelding nibbled at his jacket.

"King breeding. He is David's fallback roping horse, in case his horse can't be ridden. It has happened. David pushes his horses too hard. All for the money." She said while shaking her head in disapproval.

"He doesn't know what he has," Jamie muttered. Claire had to agree with him, but kept silent. She wasn't the kind of woman who complained, or spoke up against anyone. Not a judge, not her, because she knew everyone had their own ways, their own faults. God knew she had her own. Didn't she put her own mother in a nursing home? Didn't she let the ranch go while writing? Didn't she let Rusty get hit? Wasn't she the recluse she swore she'd never become?

"Stop, your go someplace I can't follow, stay here with me," Jamie said softly knowing that Claire's mind was wandering. "Can't you just enjoy yourself for awhile? LOOK! It's snowing!"

Claire giggled when a huge snowflake landed on her nose. She tilted her head back and caught a few on her tongue, like a child, and Jamie laughed out loud. He caught a few himself, and slapped the gelding playfully on the rump. It was a good time, although simple and quiet, and something gave way inside of Claire; the wall she had been building was crumbling, and she wasn't even aware of it.

After saddling the horses, they headed out back to the gentle hills, dusted with white. They talked of their childhoods, of horses, of writing, and about parents. They were becoming friends, and both liked the feeling. It was easy to be around each other, and you didn't meet folks like that every day.

About an hour out, he suggested that they head back, as he had to get going. Disappointed, they both were sorry to see the evening end.

After brushing the horses down and filling the feed buckets, they walked back to the house in companionable silence. Jamie fumbled for words. He wasn't a ladies man, not easy with words, but he knew he wanted to see her again. She was an orchid amid roses, and he wanted her in his life.

Standing at the front door as he was about to leave, he turned to her, cap in hand. She looked up at him with shining gray eyes, soft as a dove's down, And smiled.

"I want to thank you, Jamie," she said quietly. "In spite of the way we met, I had a wonderful evening with you. If you ever get by this way again, feel free to stop in for coffee. Maybe we can go riding again, or just talk, or something."

"I would like that," he grinned. "I would also like to re-place your Rusty for you. A gal should have a good com-panion." She looked at him quizzically, down to his boots, then back up to his face, his cheeks rosy from the cold.

"Oh, I don't know…" she murmured, straight-faced. "Would you chase 'possums out of the chicken house, and wear a flea collar?"

When it dawned on him what she meant, Jamie broke into a gut-deep laugh. He kissed her cheek and strode to his truck. He was still laughing as he pulled onto the snow-dusted road. Oh, yeah, he would see her again.

3

Aweek later, while checking her mail, she noticed a hand written envelope, not a normal site anymore, she brought it inside for better light and it was from her handsome stranger Jamie.

Dear Claire,

I wanted to say hello and to apologize again for running over Rusty. I still get a bit weepy when I think about it. I would never do anything deliberate to hurt an animal...or a person, for that matter. The offer stands to find you a new pup.

I am back at work, at the base, and have been thinking about all we talked about. It has lifted my spirits to have found someone so comfortable to be around. I usually get tongue-tied around women, but it was so darned easy to just be with you. It was great. Just wanted you to know.

I wrote to my folks and told them about you. When I said I wanted to see you again, I meant it. And when Mom wrote back, she was thrilled that I had moved on from the ended relationship I was in. She said she would love to meet you some day.

Our Irish setter had a litter of pups a couple of weeks ago. I can hardly wait to visit home to see them. Mom told me one of the pups isn't as red as the others, kind of a muted auburn, and a bit on the quiet side. The rest are deep red and roley -poley. If God made anything better than puppies and children, he must have kept it for Himself.

I get a week's leave over Christmas. I'm going home to see the folks, the pups, and hopefully...if it's OK with you, to spend some time up there with you. That sounds a bit forward, and I'm sorry if it's too soon to say so, but I would love to spend Christmas with you. What do you think? Maybe?

Sincerely, Jamie

His letters came almost daily. She flew out to the mailbox each afternoon, a giddy hope in her heart, anticipating his words of encouragement and longing. Claire was amazed that he could write what SHE felt inside. Feeling she knew him better than she ever knew David, she was finding it hard to remember what she saw in the flashy, drug-store cowboy that danced into and out of her life.

David was the only child of a wealthy ranch family over in the next county. He was raised on the best of everything, clothes, cars, horses and the admiration of all the ladies who laid eyes on him. Sure, he was very good looking, and he had a charm that he didn't mind spreading around. He WAS a top-notch rider, and he had trophies and a sizeable bank account from his success on the rodeo circuit. But he lacked the loyalty and devotion that his parents shared. He was spoiled, and expected the world to bow in his wake. He didn't understand her steadfast support of the mother she had finally had to place in a nursing home. Her weekly visits and time spent reading to Mom didn't sit well with him. Claire never faltered in the love of her parents, especially after Dad passed away. What he did want her to do? Forget about her Mom and act like she didn't exist? Wasn't going to happen, Claire thought defiantly. She had only one Mom, and being the only parent she had left, she gave her all to her. If it hadn't been for Mom wandering off, and setting the kitchen on fire when she forgot she was cooking something, the two of them would still be a family unit at home. Claire teared up as she thought of her mother's younger years… riding horses like she was born on one, always laughing, her hair blowing long and curly in the wind, the gardens and flowers all around the house, the fiddle she played so sweetly…the songs of her Scottish ancestors. The fiddle now sat, forgotten, in the pink and frilly bedroom that Claire couldn't bring herself to redecorate. Mom would never come home. Never come home. So Claire went to her. Like clockwork.

"Stop it!" she said to herself, wiping her eyes. She couldn't change what was, so she accepted, adapted, and struggled on. Alone. She sat down at her laptop and picked up the story she was writing. Soon, she was lost in a world of cities, war, and lost loves. It was what she did, and she did it well enough to make a decent living at it.

Two days before Thanksgiving, David pulled up in the driveway as she was fetching the mail. Disappointed that she would have to wait to read Jamie's letter, she walked over to the flashy silver pickup truck as David got out. He looked good, fit and happy. But not as handsome as she remembered him. She knew she would rather be seeing Jamie's face before her.

"Hello, Darlin'!" he shouted, grabbing her and swinging her around. "You're looking bright today! Where's Rusty? He didn't run out to meet me."

Her head dropped down as she felt tears rush to escape from her eyes, "Rusty got hit a few weeks ago, chasing cars again."

"Oh man that really sucks Sweetie. What's for supper?" He said nonchalantly as he hurried past her into the house.

Really? That was all? Sorry to hear that? What's for supper? Like he hadn't been gone for months, like Rusty's life meant nothing? Disgust rose up in Claire like an swirling black cloud, and she turned away so he couldn't see the anger in her eyes. And she wondered…why did she always hide her feelings from him? But she knew. She was closed to him because she knew he didn't truly deep down care. And it suddenly dawned on her. She no longer cared for him. It was well and truly over, all it took was one final encounter for her to know that she was in fact done, she didn't need this slimy worm in her life, and he was about to figure it out.

"I'm going to see Mom this afternoon and thought I would just pick up a pizza in town." Let him chew on THAT one.

"What? Is this some kind of a joke, I just get home and you're leaving? No supper, no welcome home, David? What's the matter with you?"

"I just wised up," she retorted. "No phone calls, no visits, no kiss my butt, NOTHING! I'm through waiting and wondering and spending all of my time alone, waiting for someone to care about me. Get whatever belongs to you, pack it up and get out of my house. I'm sure there are plenty of women who would jump at the chance to take my place. Ask THEM to cook for you. To wait for you. I'm done."

He looked at her as though she had lost her mind, his eyes wide and disbelieving. What kind of foolishness was this? One look at the determination in her eyes and the square set of her jaw told him, in no uncertain terms, that she meant every word she had spoken.

David shrugged his shoulders and headed into the bathroom to get the few things he had that belonged to him in her house. Oh, well, he thought, there was a saucy little blond in El Reno that would be glad to see him again. She wasn't very bright, but damn, she was good in bed. He wondered if she could cook.

Claire watched him as he loaded a bag into the bed of his truck, look at her one more time as in giving her a second chance, and then finally seeing him rev his motor and peel out of the drive away.

" What a loser." She said out loud, rolling her eyes, for once proud of herself. Little did he know that she had seen her Mom yesterday. And she would celebrate and have steak for dinner. She tore open Jamie's letter with fevered fingers. And smiled.

Dear Claire,

Work goes well. We had a company dinner planned for Thanksgiving, until seven of our men came down with the flu. Looks like it's postponed for a few days. It gives me time to write, and think. And I think about you most of the time. About how you are, what you're writing, how the weather is there, and if you're taking any time to ride. You should, you know. The joy on your face told me that riding is one of your truly enjoyable pastimes, you need to spend some time with those beautiful creatures outside.

Mom and Dad are doing well, and can't wait 'til I come home over Christmas. Which leads me to ask, how would you like to meet my folks and spend Christmas with us? Mom always makes a huge dinner and goes all out. My brothers and their families will be there, and there's plenty of room for a guest. I would love for you to see my side of family life.

I'm sure the pups will be big enough to play with, and there isn't a better anti-depressant than lying on the floor and being muggled by a whole litter of pups.

We have enough horses to ride, and you can help trim the tree on Christmas Eve. We can stop and see your mother on the way down. I would love to meet her. She must be an amazing woman. I can tell just by the daughter she raised. I have a book I bought for her. I think she would like it.

I hope you will consider it, Claire. It just won't seem complete without you. Let me know so I can make arrangements, ok?

Love, Jamie

Claire smiled as she sat down at the desk, pulled out her old yellow lined tablet and picked up her pen. An e-mail would have been faster, but snail mail had a more personal touch and he was well worth the cramp she got in her right hand when she actually did write on paper, he sure deserved that. He had picked up a book for Mom and wanted to meet her? David had NEVER showed any interest in her mother. And Christmas with Jamie's family? David had never asked her to join his family for Christmas. The difference between the two men was like night and day. She smiled again, catching herself at it. When was the last time she had smiled so much? When was the last time she had looked forward to anything? When did she fall into the trap of thinking she didn't deserve this feeling? She wondered if people built walls around their heart to keep people out, or to see who cared enough to climb them. Jamie was a climber. She smiled again, this way all the way from deep inside.

Claire knew that there were three paths that people could travel. One path was wide and well-traveled. The path of the "norm". That path so many took because what they really wanted was the typical life…love, family, success, and the so-called American dream.

The second path had side roads that branched off from the main trail, then wove in and out, away from and back to the main. It was the wonderers and thinkers, the curious and the ones thirsty for "more", but who wanted the security of the known.

The third path was blazed out of rock and timber, where no one had made a path before. These were the wanderers, the lone wolves, the seekers of the unknown, the ones who just had to see what was over the next hill, around the next bend. These were the ones who forged ahead, leaving behind security and the known, to find for themselves the answers to questions that the norm would never think to ask.

Claire thought on her own path, which one was it? Was she content with the first path? Did it hold all she ever wanted, or was she just as curious as to what lay beyond the blue and silver mountains, through the dense wild lands that held so many things that many would never see? She fit into the second path, for following the third would take her away from the ranch, away from all those she knew and loved. She wished she could take the third, but family and this ranch was in her blood, and she knew she would never wander too far from these.

It gave her pause for thought, and gave her inspiration for her writing. It didn't take long to finish her story, and she sent it off for approval. She wandered around the house for a time, deep in memories. She missed the music. The song of the trees and the horses. The cheerful chatter of birds. The music her mother played so sweetly on the fiddle. And it dawned on her. It wasn't over. There was still music, she just had to listen with her heart.

Claire grabbed her coat, her truck keys, and Mom's fiddle. Locking her door, she headed for the nursing home.

4

The residents of the nursing home had just finished dinner and were settling back into their rooms when Claire got there. Walking down the lonely hallways all she could hear was the numbing sound of televisions on just for background noise. Once she reached the end of the hall where her mothers room was located, she knocked once and slowly opened the door into her mother's room.

Sitting by the window in her favorite flannel pajamas was Claire's mother, gazing out the window at the leafless trees and the squirrels running out trying to find what little amount of nuts had found their way to the grass. Her mother turned at the sound of her footsteps, she looked at Claire and the fiddle case. Her eyes, puzzled, met Claire's.

Claire's mother was beautiful, even though time and age had taken her spark she could still take your breathe away. Her long silver hair was always neatly braided, winded at the end with a bone and leather pin, a gift she received from an Apache woman during one of her many travels. Her eyes were bluer than a Texas summer sky and just as beautiful, although recently they seemed to wander more than focus they were a sight to see none the less.

"Hello, Claire, sweet daughter. I have missed you, I feel like you never visit your old mom anymore dear." she said in her soft spoken tone. Little did her mother recall, Claire visited almost daily, but her Momma's mind was going and rarely did she remember who Claire was let alone the regularity of her visits.

A good day! Claire was heartened to be recognized, and knew it would be a fine visit, even though she had been here just two days ago. She laid the case on the bed and opened it, rosining the bow, and handed it to her mother, who took it tentatively.

"Play me a tune, Momma," Claire suggested. "I miss the sound of your music."

Taking up the instrument, putting it to her chin, her mother drew the bow across the strings. Her eyes grew bright and she spilled out a song she had often played for Claire before, when life had been sweet and normal. The notes flew like leaves in the wind, dancing and swirling through the tiny room , smooth as smoke. Claire watched intently, eyes filled with wonder just like when she was a child, as her mother played the music that had once been so important to them both. Her skill made her songs tell stories, sad and bittersweet, then upbeat and foot-tappingly lively.

It wasn't long before some of the other old folks crowded around the door, feet tapping, smiles on their faces. Claire made room for them on the bed and chairs, and saw her mother smile for the first time in a very long time. They made requests for songs they knew, and some even sang along. The head nurse came by to see what had drawn such a crowd and smiled as well. She called for coffee and cakes, which all shared as they listened to music that brought them together in the universal language. Mr. Rivers went to fetch his guitar, and Mrs. Danver came in with her tin whistle. Soon there were too many people to fit into the room, and they all moved into the day room where an upright piano sat.

Claire wished she had had a camcorder to put this on tape. The music was disjointed at times, and a wrong note could be heard occasionally, but for an impromptu get together, it sounded like heaven should sound. Angel's voices were never any sweeter. Claire felt a warmth and happiness that had been missing from her life for years. The head nurse, Mrs. Nelson, looked at the patients in her care, and felt that whatever had caused Claire to come up with this idea, it had been a fine one. She wondered if a weekly get-together would benefit the old folks as much as it had this night. That Claire was a good daughter, and the love that shown in her eyes for her mother made Mrs. Nelson glad that she was in the job she was.

Little did she know that the musical gathering would become a sweet constant in the daily lives of her patients. Not only would it be a nearly everyday event, but soon they would be giving a concert for their families as well. There was more interaction and togetherness through the music than there had ever been in the craft classes or the outings to the local eatery. Smart girl, that Claire. Wanda

Nelson wondered if she could get Claire in the payroll.

That night, back home, Claire slept better than she had in months.

Claire was not only paid for the story she wrote, but she ended up with contracts for four more. Seven hundred dollars not only paid the bills, but bought a lot of hay and grain for the horses. With a bit of breathing room, Claire decided to spend some time every day riding out into the hills, the brisk wind putting color in her cheeks and taking a bit of fat off of the lazy mare. It was a win-win situation.

Saturday morning dawned cold and crisp in spite of the sun. Bundled up warmly, with her cell phone and a lunch packed inside her saddle bags, Claire set out for the valley behind the house. The mare was glad to be out and about, and danced gaily. Claire knew she could check the fences between her ranch and the Gilbert's spread, and check the water level in the pond. It was something she hadn't done in awhile, but was pleased to see everything was in good order.

Birds followed her as she rode singing across the meadow. She missed Rusty running alongside, barking at the quail he scared up. Maybe she SHOULD think about another dog. Hadn't Jamie said a girl should have a companion? Maybe he was right. Maybe it was time to think about finding another dog. Perhaps she would check with the local rescue operation in town. There might be a good old dog in need of a home. She had the land and the love to give. Why not?

She stopped for lunch beside a small brook that cut across her land. It bubbled and gurgled over the stones and sticks that had fallen in Autumn, and Claire heard the music all around her. She made a vow that she would never close her heart to it all ever again. She had been stagnating just sitting at home. This was life. This was laughter and dreams and sheer enjoyment. Even the approaching clouds couldn't diminish the pleasure she had rediscovered. The herd of purebred Hereford cattle on the Gilbert ranch were fat and furry, ready for a harsh winter, should it get bad this year. She watched the yearlings play while their mothers grazed. Life was good. When did she forget this?

Mounting back up, Claire headed down farther into the valley. The sky was getting gray with scudding clouds, and she knew she should head back for home, but this felt so good to be back in the saddle, to be reminded that life goes on, no matter how many bumps you hit in the road. You had to take a few bumps to appreciate the good times, she reminded herself. If it was smooth sailing all of the time, one could grow complacent and take it for granted. And she never wanted that to happen.

Her horse kicked up a covey of quail, and out of high spirits and silliness, the mare shied and bolted. Lost in thought, Claire wasn't expecting the movement and slid sideways in her saddle, making the mare buck frivolously. Claire hit the ground hard on her shoulder and left knee. The mare ran off towards home, probably laughing at her, Claire thought grumpily. When she tried to rise, her knee buckled and a horrendous pain left her head swirling. She knew she wasn't walking home. She thought about her cell phone, but it was in her saddle bag on the damned horse. She cursed the horse, then cursed her luck. The she tried again to get to her feet. Her knee gave way and sent her into waves of pain. Then the panic set in. She looked around and realized that the house was three miles away. And it was getting cold. Looking at the clouds, she saw that snowflakes were coming down. A fine mess, she frowned, thinking of the turkey set out on the countertop to start thawing. It was crawl or freeze, she knew. But when she tried to crawl on her hands and knees, the pain was more than she could bear. She sat down on her backside and cried.

After a twenty minute session of feeling sorry for herself, she tried to clear her mind, knowing she could be in a serious predicament if she didn't get going. It would be dark in an hour or so, and with the darkness the cold would become dangerous. She unconsciously pulled her jacket collar up and rewrapped her scarf around her face and neck. Pulling on her gloves, Claire looked around in hopes that someone might be within shouting distance. No such luck. The Gilberts were probably sitting by their fireplace, talking of Christmas preparations. The mare was nowhere to be seen, and the snow was falling thicker and faster.

A crutch. She needed a crutch. Glancing around her, she spotted a large branch lying on the ground about thirty yards from her. Scooting on her rump, she slowly and painfully made her way over to it. Standing it upright, Claire tried to pull herself up on it, only to have the dead, brittle branch break and send her back to the frozen dirt and leaves, more pain shooting up her leg and shoulder. The darkness was roaring in, and Claire knew she may have to spend the night out here. It was a dismal thought, even being bundled up in woolies and layers, and she almost broke down again into tears.

There is, in all women, a sense of survival. It causes them to take a deep breath, use their brain, and climb what seems to most to be an insurmountable mountain. It draws from an ancient time when women weren't strangers to hard lives, when they were wild and strong and as fierce as men. A primal heat that provides the strength to kick ass when needed. It was this fierceness that propelled Claire to keep moving, to seek shelter from the elements. Up the hill behind her was a patch of cedar trees, bunched close enough to provide a break from the bitter wind. It was there Claire headed, slowly inching her way like a worm. By the time she reached the trees, she was done. Her strength was gone, and she was colder than she had ever been in her life. She scooped dead leaves around her for insulation, pulled her scarf over her face and head, and passed out.

Jamie looked in on the sickly men in his unit, giving

comfort when he could, trying to bolster their morale on the holiday missed. Claire was front and center in his mind, never more than a thought away, and he missed her gentleness, her infrequent but shining smile. He knew his parents would see what he saw in her, the loyalty to family, the readiness to work hard to keep the ranch up, the pleasure she took from the simplest of things. Again he thought what a fool this David person was. He had thrown away a diamond. How could one man be so blind?

Bringing Claire to Christmas at his folk's house really gave him something to look forward to. He was excited at the prospect of seeing her again, but also the thought of his Mom and Dad meeting her made him happy deep down inside. He could actually see a future with this woman, and that surprised him. He didn't think he would ever think like that again. Maybe he should call her, just to say good-night. He had thought of calling her several times, but hesitated at the thought of disturbing her while she was writing. Surely she wouldn't be writing this late? Their letters back and forth brought him an odd sense of comfort. Being out in the field so much, e-mails weren't always possible, and hand written letters were something he would keep forever. Forever…what an exciting thought.

He reached for the phone on his desk, dialed her number, and leaned back in his chair while it rang. And rang. And rang. No answer. Maybe she was already in bed. He hoped everything was alright at the ranch, and OK with her Mom. Oh, well, he'd try again tomorrow. He turned off the light and headed for his barracks. He wondered how he could feel like this, after being deserted by his fiancé. It had taken the wind out of his sails for a long time, and he had no plans to care about any woman again.

He tried to watch a movie, but missed most of it while thinking about Claire. He really liked the unassuming way she had of looking at things, and felt bad that life had handed her so much less than she deserved. She wasn't bitter, or jaded, as she could have been. She accepted her lot in life and kept going. There was so much that he wanted to give her, to enjoy with her, but most of all, he wanted to see that smile on a regular basis. Oh, yeah, he had it bad for this quiet girl who spoke not enough and smiled even less.

Claire awoke before dawn, so cold that her teeth were chattering as violently as her body was shaking. Six inches of snow had dropped since she had lain down under the cedars, and even the layers of leaves she had pulled over herself hadn't keep the snow from seeping in and wetting her clothes. She knew if she didn't get home, and soon, she never would.

Rubbing her arms and legs briskly, she again stirred the pain that almost sent her over the edge. She wondered vaguely if she had broken her leg. Her shoulder was sore as hell, but she could move it and raise her arm, so it didn't seem too bad. Her leg was another story. Her foot was so swollen that it puffed out over the top of her boot. She had to get moving before hypothermia set in, if it hadn't already.

She pulled herself up on the branches of the cedar, wincing at the awful pain in her leg, as she tried to stand on just the good one. A tentative step on the bad one told her that nothing had changed, she still couldn't walk. Well, then, she'd just have to crawl. And crawl she did. Through the snow. And each inch found the cold white crap filling every opening in her clothes with wet snow. So she brushed away the snow with her arms before she inched forward, slowly, ever so slowly, and kept thinking about the turkey thawing on the counter. If she didn't make it home soon, it would spoil and leave an awful stench in the house. Raising up on her good arm, she looked around to see if anyone was around. There was nothing but silence, cold and threatening silence. She started to crawl again. She tried to think about summer, warm and sunny, when she would fix fence and grow vegetables and mow her yard. That would be nice. Oh, yes, even as big as her yard was, mowing would be nice right now.

Coming up on the brook where she had eaten her lunch, she wanted to take a drink. The water was probably not clean enough to drink, and it would be cold. She didn't need to lose anymore body heat, so she passed up the drink, and crawled across the moving water, thoroughly wetting her. The deadliness of her situation was dawning on her big time, and terror set in, even knowing how defeating that fright could be. She had to keep a clear head and not panic. Surely when the sun came up, someone would see her and come to help. Maybe the Gilberts would be out bringing hay to the cattle. She would keep a look out for any sound or movement as she crawled forward. Just keep going, she ordered herself. Keep moving. It DID bring back a bit of warmth to her body, except the wetness from the creek sapped it as soon as she generated it. If she lived through this, she would never take heat for granted again. Or warm showers, or a hot meal. Food, she thought. Food. Yesterday's unfinished picnic lunch had consisted of a sandwich and a bottle of tea. What she would give for that uneaten portion now.

Jamie tried calling her again at 8:30 that morning. Still no answer. What the hell? He did paper work until 9:30, then tried to reach her a second time. Nothing. He got an uneasy feeling in his stomach, and tried again at 10:00. Again it went to voice mail. He left a brief request for her to call him, then looked up the number for the only nursing home in her town. Calling THAT number, he learned that Claire wasn't supposed to be in for a visit until Wednesday, but that her mother was fine, even more chipper and aware than usual. He smiled when Mrs. Nelson told him about Claire bringing in her mother's fiddle, and the ensuing get together. He wished he could have been there. He left with Mrs. Nelson promising to have Claire call him if she showed up there. He sat down to write another letter. Maybe it was too soon to feel this way about her, but he wasn't as foolish as David. He put his heart and soul into the letter, taking his time to let her know just how much he had come to care about her.

Claire couldn't feel her feet or legs anymore. Her face felt like frozen meat, and she was running out of steam. And she was tired. So very tired. Maybe just a quick nap, to build up some stamina. She looked around once more, praying to see someone, anyone, but the valley lay cold and white and very empty. She put her head down onto her arms, and drifted off as tears fell down her cold face.

She dreamed. The convoluted dreams of the exhausted, the badly hurt, the dreams of someone falling into hypothermia. She was laying on the bank of the pond, basking in the sun, listening to the birds and feeling her skin tan. She could taste the apple she was munching on, and the juice dribbled down her cheek. She brushed at it absently and turned over…and came face to face with the biggest rabbit she had ever seen. It smiled at her and wiggled it's whiskers. Then it spoke, showing it's buck teeth and wiggling it's ears.

"What are you doing, silly woman?" it queried.

"I'm soaking up the sun and enjoying myself. What are YOU doing?"

"You're laying in the water. Why?" The rabbit cocked it's head to one side and one ear flopped down.

"Because I'm waiting for a ride," Claire replied drowsily.

"Your ride has been standing here for hours," the rabbit said haughtily. "Shouldn't you go?"

Claire woke up and winced at the pain shooting through her body. The mare was nuzzling Claire's cheek and puffed warm air against her forehead. She had come back. Claire squinted against the foggy breath, suddenly aware that she was alive, no longer alone and had a chance to get home. She reached for the reins with a frozen hand and found she couldn't get her fingers to close around the leather straps. Here was an offer of salvation and she couldn't grab it.

The warrior in Claire refused to give up.

"MOVE!" she told herself. "DO something!"

She reached up with her good arm and hooked it through the stirrup dangling above her. Every bone in her body felt as though it were broken and useless, but she managed to hold tight with her elbow. The mare moved off a step, dragging Claire across the ground, across the frozen dirt and leaves. They moved another step. Claire held on doggedly, wanting to scream with every movement. Then another step, and another. Progress was infuriatingly slow, but it WAS movement, and they were heading for the home place.

After not being able to get hold of Claire by phone, Jamie started to panic. He called the sheriff in Claire's town and told him that Claire may be in trouble, could someone please go out and check on her. The sheriff, friends with Claire's parents for years, agreed to send someone out to the ranch.

Deputy Frank Sellers had had a silent crush on Claire for years. Frank was a shy, gangly man, not comfortable around the ladies, and therefore never let his feelings be known. He hopped at the chance to go out and see her again. Driving down the dirt road now covered with sparkling snow, he wondered if she was still seeing that good for nothing cowboy that slept with every girl he could. Frank really disliked men who used women like that. Women were made to be protected and cherished, like his dad took care of his mother. Now, THAT was how a couple should be. Close. Caring. Raising kids with love and laughter. That is how he would have treated Claire, if he had had the balls to ask her out.

There were no tracks in the snow on Claire's road. No one had been in or out since last night at least. She was probably holed up against the cold, staying indoors like a any sensible person would do. He pulled into the driveway and was greeted by the gelding's impatient whinny, it's head bobbing up and down and pawing at the snow. There weren't even any tracks leading to or from the barn, and the animals were obviously hungry. Walking up the steps to the house, Frank noticed that there was no smoke coming from the chimney. He knew Claire's father had installed a sweet wood burning stove before he died, and they used it more than the electric furnace.

Peeking in the window, he saw no movement of any kind. Frank knocked on the door loudly, but there was no sound. No one came to the door. So he trudged through the snow to each window, thinking she may be in the back. No one was in the house.

The next logical place to check would be the barn. Maybe Claire was out there and laying hurt, unable to get to the house. The barn door swung wide, and several cats cam begging for food.

"Claire!" Frank hollered. "Are you in here?" It was silent except for the hungry felines, now trying to climb his legs. He reached down and petted a couple, then walk to his truck and got on the radio.

"Sheriff, there is no one here," he told Sheriff MacClellan. "I checked the house and the barn, and she hasn't been out since it snowed. No prints anywhere."

"Check the back door, see if it's locked, and if you can get in, go in, room by room. If it's locked, jimmy it. We need to find her. Is her truck there?"

"Yup, it's next to the house. Hasn't been driven, either."

"Get into that house. Check it out and let me know."

"Right," Frank answered.

The back door was unlocked, not unusual for this part of the county. No one bothered each other, and the crime rate was almost zilch out here. Frank went in, wiping his boots and pulling off his winter cap. He went to the back of the house first, where he had been unable to see in through the windows there. It was empty of life, eerily silent. Claire's bed was made, the room was neat, and he paused for a moment at a picture of Claire and her parents in a elegant silver frame. It was a photo of a family the way a family should be, smiling, loving and close. A photo of before sadness struck with it's evil breath. Frank shook his head sadly and moved to the other rooms, all as empty as the previous one.

When he got to the kitchen, Frank noticed a turkey sitting on the counter next to the sink. He put his hand on it, and felt that it was almost thawed out. Without a second thought, he picked it up and put it in the refrigerator. Now he was really worried. Rusty was gone, as well. Everyone knew Rusty, the duck chaser, the car chaser, the big friendly Golden Retriever with the goofy grin and constantly wagging tail.

Frank called back in and reported his lack of findings. Then he headed down to the Parnell spread to see if they had heard from her. No one had, and now it looked as though they had a missing person to find.

Sheriff MacClellan called Jamie as soon as Frank talked to the Parnells. He was going to call together a few people to look for Claire. Jamie's heart plummeted to his feet. The taste of fear was bitter in his mouth. He called his C.O. and requested a week off. When his commanding officer heard what was going on, he granted Jamie his leave and wished him well. Jamie was packed and out the door in less than ten minutes.

Jamie met Sheriff MacClellan as soon as he roared into town. He knew had broken every speed limit between his base and here, not to mention driving in some unsafe and very slick conditions. The sooner he got there, he figured, the sooner he could do something other than worry himself sick.

They drove out to the ranch in the Sheriff's squad car and parked near the house. Getting out, they threw on bulky coats and gloves against the cold. The only tracks to be found had been made by Frank in his search. Jamie's heart felt as cold as the weather. Where had she gone that she had left no tracks? Had someone kidnapped her before the snow covered everything up? Why would they do that? She had so money to speak of, ransom wouldn't make any sense. Had she gone somewhere with David? David! Why hadn't he thought of her being with David?

"Sheriff, do you know where David lives? I don't know his last name, but he comes around every so often to see Claire."

David Saunders," Frank said with distaste. "He lives over in the next county. I'll give him a call."

Jamie went outside and walked towards the barn. The cats swarmed around him, wanting a meal, and he walked to the feed room to get some cat food for them. Frank walked in behind him and told him that David hadn't seen her since she sent him packing a few days ago. Jamie didn't know whether to be pleased that she had dumped David, or to worry because he had hoped they had been together and now that was one option to not be considered.

He walked outside, scratching his head. Where the hell could she be? Frank followed him, every bit as puzzled.

"I couldn't even find Rusty," Frank told him. "Rusty is always with her when he isn't chasing ducks. There weren't even any dog tracks around here."

So Jamie told Frank about Rusty's death, and how that was how he had met Claire. She was out there somewhere, God knew where, and he was here with his hands tied, his heart hurting, and his mind whirling in fear. When the gelding came up to the fence to greet him, he knew the horse must be hungry as well, so he went back into the barn and broke open a square bale of hay and got a can of sweet feed to take back out. Holding several flakes of hay in one arm and the can of feed in the other, he kicked the snow away from the feed bucket and dumped it in. The hay he tossed next to it. The gelding bend his head down eagerly and began to eat. Jamie patted him absently, when it dawned on him that the mare wasn't with the gelding. He walked out into the pen and looked around. The mare was gone. That meant that Claire had gone riding. Jamie hollered for the other men.

"Her mare is gone!" he shouted. "She went riding and hasn't come back!"

"She hasn't been out here, riding, all this time," Frank answered. "She's got to be out there and hurt!"

"We've got to find her!" Jamie cried. "She could be laying out there in the cold! Sheriff MacClellan, get to the neighboring ranches and have them check around to see if they have seen her. I'm going to saddle the gelding and take him out. If you hear anything, or anyone finds her, shoot once. I'll hear it. It will echo across these hills."

Jamie ran into the barn, grabbed a saddle and blanket, and a bridle that looked as though it would fit the bigger animal's head. He saddle up in spite of the horse wanted to finish it's meal. He opened the gate, leaving it open, for there was nothing left to keep in. Swinging his lanky frame up onto the horse's back, he kicked it into gear and galloped off to the back of the ranch. There was a lot of land to cover, and he had no idea which way she had gone, but it was better than standing around, worrying.

Claire held on to the stirrup, unaware of anything around her except for the horse dragging her painfully across the frozen snow, one slow step after another. Time no longer existed for her, just the steady movement that wracked her with pain, reminding her that she was still alive. She wondered if dying would hurt this much. Maybe it would be easier to just let go, to just fall asleep and forget everything. She almost did let go, once, until Jamie's face came to her. He was smiling that tender smile of his, looking at her with those ocean-blue eyes. Oh, how she wanted to see those gorgeous blue eyes just one more time. He would make everything better, she just KNEW it! So, she held on, and closed her eyes, feeling the mare trying to take her home. Home. Home was warm. Home was safe. Home was Jamie.

Christmas is a special time, not only in the Biblical sense, but in the way it has of bringing people together. It isn't so much about the presents under the tree, but the about people who came together with love. It was about family and friends, closeness, good times shared, good food shared, and a sense of belonging somewhere. It is enhanced with colored lights, frenzied wrapping of gifts at the last moment, and fathers trying to put together bikes and toys without looking at the directions, then wishing they had. It is the laughter, the anticipation of the children, the use of the usual threat of Santa not coming if the kids are still awake. But, the bottom line, the most important part of the day was love.

Jamie was determined to have Claire with him this Christmas. It was the greatest gift he could think of. Not much else mattered. Without her, he wouldn't have cared if he had to stay on base and work. He wanted to see the expression on her face when she opened her first gift that he had for her. It had taken some doing, going to the library, searching through years of newspapers, to find a picture of her parents, together. It had taken three trips before he found one, posted along with an article about how Jamie's folks had donated enough money to build a playground at Claire's old school. It was just a black and white photo, to put into a sliver locket on a chain. He had noticed that Claire preferred silver to gold, and he hoped she would like it. The second gift would be the best. He grinned as he thought of it. What would she do when she opened THAT one?

He was still riding the hills behind the ranch when he decided to move lower into the valley. Trying to think as she would, Jamie studied the land. He knew she was bright and capable, and she knew the land better than anyone except for her father, long gone. He watched the ground, hoping for a sign of movement, a track, a broken twig, anything that would say that someone had been there lately. There was nothing, nothing that wasn't covered by the cold white blanket of the last snow. In his frustration, he kicked the gelding into a canter, moving back and forth every twenty or thirty feet, casting for some sign of passage. Damn it, where was she? Was she even out here? Where could she have gone?

Frank and the sheriff went to the Parnell's and the Gilbert's to enlist their help in searching for Claire. Everyone knew and thought highly of the young woman, and sprang into action. Steve Parnell fired up his snowmobile and headed out, while Martin Gilbert started up his truck to check his back acreage that bordered on Claire's land. Sheriff MacClellan drove back to town to handle another emergency, but left Frank at Claire's to make coffee and to keep in touch by radio should anyone find Claire.

Frank felt odd going through Claire's cabinets, looking for coffee and filters, but he knew they would need something to warm themselves when they came back to the house. He was afraid, afraid of what they would find, or more so what would happen if they didn't find anything. Why hadn't he had the guts to ask Claire out? Why hadn't he let his feelings be known?

He looked at her kitchen, neat and clean and inviting. You could tell a lot about a woman by looking at her kitchen. It was obvious that Claire loved to cook; there were a variety of pans and utensils hanging on the wall rack and gathered neatly in jugs, cabinets full of baking pans and gadgets. And it was well organized, everything within reach of a pair of busy hands. The windows weren't covered by curtains, just decorative valances that left a nice view of the ranch. It was clear that someone who loved the land lived here. He wished he had gotten the chance to know her better. Even though David was out of the picture, it was obvious to Frank that Jamie was in love with Claire, and he felt he would never be able to compete with someone like the tall, handsome Marine. It didn't matter, he told himself. All he wanted right now was for Claire to found and for her to be alright.

Claire was past feeling anything. She wasn't really even cold anymore. She was still aware of every step the mare made, gently dragging her towards home, and her eyes closed as she concentrated on simply hanging on. She remembered her father dragging her around on a sled behind his horse, the way she used to laugh when she hit a bump and went flying upward. She could hear his laughter as the horse occasionally kicked up puffs of snow into her grinning face. Afterward, back at the house, they would share hot chocolate and cinnamon buns, fresh from her mother's oven. Oh, what she would give for one of those sticky, sweet buns right now, covered with white icing. Mom. Was it today that she was supposed to go visit her mother? What day was this? And where was Rusty? She would give anything to have Rusty running alongside, tongue lolling as he grinned at her. Probably chasing Mr. Gilbert's ducks on the pond again. Silly dog. Didn't he know he would never be able to catch them?

She thought she was dreaming when she heard the mare whinny. Surely it was a dream. She was home, in bed, and all she wanted to do was sleep. Then the mare whinnied again, and the sound of pounding hooves broke through to her.

Jamie saw the mare before he saw Claire. Galloping furiously up to the riderless horse, he finally saw what the mare was dragging. Heart in his throat, he threw himself off the big gelding and gathered Claire into his arms. Oh, God, it was too late! Her eyes were closed and she was stiff with the cold. Her lips were blue and there was no response.

"NOOO!" he screamed. "NO!"

It wasn't until he tried to unhook her arm from the saddle that he found any sign of life. Claire moaned and refused to give up her grip on the stirrup, though she didn't open her eyes. She had to hang on until the mare got her home, she just had to get back to the ranch.

"CLAIRE! Claire, can you hear me?" Jamie shook her.

"Home," she mumbled. "Gotta get home."

OK, Honey, hold on. We're going home. Hang in there, it will be alright now. I've got you!"

Jamie had a hard time gathering her into his arms, as stiff as she was, but he held her tightly against him and swung up on the big gelding, Holding Claire on his lap, against his body, he kicked the horse into action, and the big dun took off like the devil had bitten him on the rump. It was smooth pasture land and the horse took it effortlessly, but it was still two and a half miles from the house. Jamie looked down at Claire's face, frightened by her lack of color, and the non-responsive way she sat in his arms.

Looking out the back window, Frank didn't see anything. It had been three hours since the search party had gone out, and there hadn't been any word from anyone of them. Not a religious man, he found himself praying, in humble but sincere words, and he was promising all kinds of things if Claire could just be home and OK.

He turned the coffee pot back on, hoping someone would be here to need it. It was extremely hard just sitting here, waiting, when he wanted to be out searching for her himself. He felt ineffectual, and helpless, and he didn't like it one bit. He walked out the back door and lit a cigarette. His only bad habit, and he didn't want to smoke in Claire's house. God, it was cold out here. He stamped his feet and rubbed his arms, though it didn't ease the cold very much. Sure was quiet without Rusty running around, barking and acting foolish.

He looked up at some birds, sitting in the tree near the back deck, and saw they were all puffed up against the icy wind. He knew how they felt. He flipped his cigarette out into the snow before he even thought, and was about to go out and grab the butt to throw it away when he noticed movement at the top of the back hill. Jamie was riding as fast as the horse could go, and Claire was in his arms. He grabbed the walkie from his belt and shouted excitedly into it.

"Jamie found her, Sheriff! They're riding in now. She doesn't look good, but he wouldn't be pushing the horse that hard if she…if…Oh, God! She has to be alive! I think you'd better send the paramedics out here, right now!"

"Will do, Frank. Fire a round off to let everyone know she's been found."

Frank unbuckled his pistol and fired a shot off into

the air. Running back into the house, he grabbed a blanket off the back of the sofa and ran out to meet them. Jamie pulled the horse to a sliding stop and slid to the ground, running for the house. Frank held open the door and closed it behind them, glad he had turned the coffee back on.

Jamie laid Claire on the sofa, covered her with a second blanket, and thought back on the training he had received in the Corp on just how to treat frostbite and hypothermia. He remembered that the core heat was all important, and he asked Frank to try to find something to make a hot broth with.

Claire's clothes were frozen solid to her, but Jamie knew he had to get them off of her. He ran to the kitchen, fumbled through a couple of drawers until he found a pair of scissors, and ran with them back to the living room and started to cut her frozen jeans from her. After the jeans were off, he pulled her coat off and snipped her blouse away. Tucking the blankets securely around her, he placed a pillow under her feet and pulled her boots off, then her wool socks. Her little toes on both feet were black, and Jamie knew that wasn't a good sign. She may lose those two little toes. If she lost her big toes, she may have to learn to walk all over again. The loss of little pinkies, while helpful with balance, wouldn't prevent her from being able to walk.

Frank came in with a cup of chicken flavored broth, and handed it to Jamie, who put it up to Claire's lips. There was no response, so he forced her mouth open gently, and poured a sip in. Claire swallowed instinctually, then coughed it up, but he made her sip some more. This time she kept a little bit down. Looking up at Jamie, she gave him a vague frown.

"Are you really here? Where are we?"

"You are home, Claire, and you're in serious shape. The paramedics are on their way. We have to get you to the hospital."

Her head sank back into the pillows and her eyes closed. She was starting to hurt all over, making Jamie wish he could do more to ease her pain. Frank brought a pan of cool water in and put her hands in it. Hot water would have made her scream, and it wasn't good to use it so soon. He bathed her face with a cool rag, and Jamie went to heat a blanket up in the microwave. Looking at her blue lips, Frank had to wonder how long she had been out there. Her skin was white, her eyes sunken in, and she was beginning to shiver violently. He wished the paramedics would hurry.

Jamie came back and wrapped the now warm blanket around her. He forced a another sip of broth down her. He and Frank exchanged worried frowns. It didn't look good. They both knew she wasn't out of the woods yet, just because she was home. Her body was shaking and she whimpered.

Suddenly, she went into convulsions. Claire's body arched and she screamed. The pain was so intense that she finally passed out, her limbs falling slack. Frank continued to hold her hands in the cool water, and wondered how she had survived out there. How long had she been lying there in the cold?

There was a knock at the door and Frank let the paramedics in and led them to Claire. They checked her pulse, lifter her eyes, and fit a blood pressure cuff around her arm. One of the men was hooking up an I.V., but had a difficult time getting the needle into her vein. She needed to be warm on the inside, more so than the outside, and the warm saline drip would help with that. He finally hit a vein and he taped the needle to her arm. His partner was calling into the hospital with Claire's vital signs, alerting them to her condition…what had been done, and what they were doing now. ETA at the hospital would be at least twenty minutes.

They loaded her onto the stretcher, raised it, and tucked the blankets firmly around her. Jamie insisted on riding with them, and Frank remained behind to turn off the coffee pot and to unsaddle the gelding, brush him down and see that he got to eat. He scooped out some more food for the barn cats, enough to hold them over for a couple of days, and hung the saddle and bridle back up. He returned to the house, made sure everything was off, locked the front door, then went out the back. He drove to the hospital to check on Claire, leaving the ranch as silent as when he first arrived. The frozen, crunchy snow broke beneath each step, and with it, broke his heart.

The doctor was hesitant to give a good report when Claire was still in critical condition. Her shoulder was dislocated, her leg was broken near the knee joint, and the MRI showed extensive tendon and ligament damage. It would be a awhile before she would be able to walk, if she came out of the coma. They had an orthopedic surgeon on staff, one of the best in the state, who would work on her leg. He told Frank the truth of the situation and went back to work. Frank located Jamie in the waiting room, just sitting down, his head in his hands. This was the stuff nightmares were made of. They both sat in silence, sipping tasteless but scalding coffee. Frank was glad that, if Claire had to be involved with someone, it was Jamie, not David. David hadn't even showed up to help search for Claire. David was a self-serving jerk, and didn't come close to deserving her affection.

However, Frank had a job to do, and got up to leave. He shook hands with Jamie, asking him to keep in touch with him if there were any changes. Walking out of the hospital, Frank wondered about the twists and turns that life through at a person. So many 'what ifs'. So much unfair trouble. Well, such was life. You made your way the best you could, and accepted the bad with the good, hoping there was enough good to outbalance the bad.

Back in the hospital waiting room, Jamie was thinking

along the same lines. How could someone, like David, lead a life of no care, stepping on folks as he did, and fall into a pile of dung, yet come out smelling like roses. Here was a lady who followed the rules, cared for others, gave of herself to so many, and trouble seemed to bark at her heels with every step. Damn, it just wasn't fair. And she lived out there, all alone, running a small ranch on her own, working from home, visiting her mother with regularity, and earning the respect of all who knew her. What more could be expected of someone?

He made up his mind that she wouldn't have to do it all alone if she pulled out of this. It was too soon to think along those lines, but his heart told him that she was the one he wanted. He hoped the feeling would be mutual. If it wasn't, he would do everything in his power to change her mind. Even if it meant chasing 'possums out of the chicken house and wearing a flea collar.

Claire had fallen into a coma, hooked up to lines that kept her hydrated and, for the most part, pain-free. Jamie never left her side, holding her hand and talking to her, first begging her to hang on, to come back to them, then speaking of little things, anything to break through to her. He spoke of the ranch, how the horses were fine, how the other animals were fed and safe. He wondered if anyone had informed her mother of the events of the last few days, but it wouldn't do any good to worry the woman. If Claire didn't come out of the coma, however, she would have the right to know. Jamie made a mental note, promising to visit the woman soon to tell her. He had been wanting to meet her anyway, to tell her how much he cared about her daughter, and that he wanted her permission to ask Claire to marry him. She was the only parent of the woman he loved, and it was to the mother that Jamie would have to go.

The doctor came out the next morning, and asked if her family was there. Jamie informed him that her only close relative was her mother, living in town at the elderly care facility. He added, although a bit prematurely, that he was Claire's fiancé. That allowed her doctor to talk to him, to tell him what must be done, and what to expect.

"She has suffered severe frostbite, as well as hypothermia. She will probably lose her little toes, as well as a bit off the top of her ears. We are working on her fingers. I expect we can wait a day or so to see if we can save them. She is still in a coma, which may be for the best right now. Her core temp has come up to ninety-six, which is very good, under the circumstances, but we need to remove the toes as soon as possible. As she is in no condition to agree to the surgery, we need someone to sign papers to allow us to remove them."

Jamie's heart skipped a couple of beats at the prospect of authorizing a procedure that could be so life-changing. Yet he knew, if it wasn't done, she would have no life. He agreed to sign the necessary forms and went up the nurse's station to fill them out. He hoped Claire would understand.

It wasn't long after he signed the papers that they came to take her up to surgery. He followed along, being shown were to wait, and sat miserably alone in the waiting room. He read every magazine on the tables, made a call to Frank to tell him of the updates, and called his C.O. to let him know what was going on. After that, he just sat, elbows on his knees, head in his hands, and prayed.

Times of tragedy have a way of pulling people together. Suddenly, it is not him and her, you and me, or them. It becomes "us", and there are no boundaries, no dividing lines. Everyone comes to the front and works to make it better for all. It's a shame that it takes a tragedy to accomplish this, and we should learn from it, living our lives in such a way that we are always looking out for one another, always willing to lend a hand without being asked.

The Parsons came by as did the Gilberts, along with the sheriff's wife and many others who had heard of Claire's misfortune. Food was brought up to the hospital for Jamie, Frank came to sit with him on his off hours, and Claire's room was filling up with cards and flowers of all types and colors; bright, vibrant shades of red and pink and yellow decorated her room as well as 'Get well soon' balloons that floated and bobbed with the air currents. It looked as though a circus had blown through and left it's best parts for her.

After four hours in surgery, Claire was brought into the recovery room, where Jamie sat beside her, her hand in his, talking to her, telling her of the well wishes of the community, of the gifts and flowers of roses and daisies, lilies and babies breath in bright glass vases.

Her skin was pale and translucent, deep shadows around her closed eyes, and her hair hung limp and lifeless. The blankets were warm, her hands bandaged, and tubes seemed to be sticking out of her in so many places. Jamie had never known such terror, and such helplessness. All he could do was be there for her, talking to her, holding her bandaged hand. He begged her to wake up, begged her to say something, to be on the road back. He knew he had to get back to base soon, and he didn't want to leave without her waking up, without knowing he was right there with her. He slept in the chair beside her bed when they took her back to her room. He was wearing the same dirty clothes as when he had found her and brought her back to the ranch. Frank was kind enough to bring him a change of clothes as they were about the same size, although Frank was bit slimmer than Jamie, and the shirt was a tight fit. Jamie's muscular body seemed to threaten to split the shirt at the seems. The hospital allowed him to shower and brought him a disposable razor, and though he was reluctant to leave Claire's side even for a short time, he felt immensely better once he cleaned up.

The day nurse came in and took Claire's vitals, pleased with her temperature and heart rate, but her blood pressure was low as was her white cell count. She fed Claire's lunch to her through a tube into her stomach, washed her face, brought fresh, warmed blanket in to replace the cool one, and patted Jamie on the shoulder as she started to leave.

"Keep talking to her, Son," she nodded. "You may not think she hears you, but we know that sometimes they do, and it is a comfort to them."

Yes, Ma'am," he said softly, tears spilling from his eyes.

The day came that Jamie had to return home to base. Claire was still comatose, and unaware that the physical therapist was exercising her legs daily, sometimes with the electric TENS machine, sometimes by hand, bending her leg to keep it limber, to avoid a build up of lesions on the scar tissue where the surgeon had to open up her leg to fix the anterior cruciate ligament and the tendons that had torn apart in the fall. He watched as the bandages were changed on her feet, catching his breath as the noticed the slender feet minus the pinky toes. He was thankful that the other toes were savable. At least she would be able to walk, whenever it was possible.

He packed up his few collected belongings, talked briefly with the nurses, and went back to tell Claire that he would be back as soon as he could, then bent to whisper in her ear.

"I love you, Claire. With all of my heart. Don't forget about Christmas, now. You are coming down to Texas with me to meet the folks. I expect you to be up and about when I come to get you." There was no response, but he somehow he knew she heard him. It was one of the hardest things he had ever done, walking out of the hospital without Claire by his side. In desolation, he pulled away and headed back for Texas.

After a week and a half of Claire's being in a coma, they began to worry. She was healing as well as could be expected, and they were puzzled at her lingering state. They were wondering what kind of stimuli would get through to her. Even though Jamie called every day, twice a day, and the nurse put the phone up to her ear, she showed no sign of joining the conscious world.

She swam in a haze of opiate bliss, feeling no pain, having not a care in the world, no longer cold, no longer afraid. She didn't want to ever leave the little island of drug-induced comfort. She had no thoughts of her mother, the ranch, Rusty, or any of the chores she had loved doing. The loneliness was gone, the darkness was not empty, filled with whirls of smoke and haze. In here there was no noise, no discomfort, no worry. There was just peaceful silence, not even a voice telling her to wake up, wake up.

The doctors decided to reduce the morphine drip. Maybe it would help to bring her back to the world. Still she slept the sleep of pseudo death, unwilling to face whatever the world held for her.

Jamie called the nursing home and told them of Claire's condition, and why she hadn't been by for her regular visits to her mother. Mrs. Nelson, the head nurse at the old folks home, had an idea. She placed a call to the hospital, and asked if it would be possible to bring her patients down for a brief concert. Not only would it be a good outing for her charges, but maybe, just maybe, Claire would hear her mother's fiddle music and come out of her present state. It was agreed upon, and scheduled for the next evening. It was time to tell Claire's mother that her daughter was in trouble and needed her.

The next evening, Claire's mother showed up, along with Mr. Rivers and Mrs. Danver, and they sat down in Claire's room and opened up the cases of their instruments. After a few tuning strokes, the music started, sweet and clear. The first song was an upbeat jig, and had everyone's toes tapping. It was a song of cheer and happiness. The nurse saw no change in Claire, although her heart rate had increased considerably. She was hearing the music! Jamie, on the phone long distance, heard the nurse encourage them to play another song. This time, it was the one tune that always enthralled Claire when her mother performed it. "She Moved Through the Fair" floated slowly through the room, whispering like the smoke from a campfire, touching every heart with it's melody.

The nurse kept watching Claire and alternately, her machine and it's readings. She put a pressure cuff on Claire's arm, and was excited to see her blood pressure rising closer to normal numbers. She relayed the news to Jamie, who quivered with the good news, and started to cry, tears running down his cheeks unchecked.

"Wake up, Honey, wake up! Hear the music!" he whispered into the phone.

"Mom?" Claire spoke faintly, but they heard it, and they all cheered loudly enough to scare the dead. Claire's mother kept playing, tears in her eyes, and gave the song every thing she had in her to give. The solo performance was every bit as beautiful as any popular violin player could play, and everyone had tears of joy in their eyes as Claire opened her eyes and looked up at the nurse.

"Is my mother here?" she asked weakly. She raised her hand as though to touch her mother, and the nurse nodded, smiling from ear to ear.

"Yes, darling, she is. And Jamie is on the phone, waiting to hear how you are."

"Jamie? My Jamie?" And when Jamie heard that, his face split into the biggest grin he had ever given anyone. Oh, yeah, she would be his Claire, to have and to hold, to cherish and protect. Life was suddenly bright and sweet and he was filled with anticipation like he had never known.

Eight days later, Claire was allowed to leave the hospital. Jamie was right there to pick her up. They laughed together as they puzzled out how they were going to get all of the flowers and balloons into his truck. There was room in the back for the wheel chair that had to be rented for awhile, as Claire wasn't allowed to walk yet. They stuffed as many of the plants as would fit into the back seat of the crew cab, then donated the leftover flowers and balloons to other patients, especially the children who were in the hospital for various reasons.

Driving out to Claire's ranch, she was excited to see the horses. She had accepted the news of her missing toes without a blink, just so very glad to be alive. She held no animosity towards the mare. There wasn't a mean bone in the horse's body, and the fall hadn't been her fault. Jamie had to carry her in his arms out to the barn, where the cats jumped up into her lap and rubbed all over her, purring and letting her know how much they had missed her. It was a load that strained his arms, but it was a sweet and precious feeling to hold her safe.

The Gilberts had been taking care of the animals for her, and all was well with all the livestock. Claire would have to bake them something special when she was able, to thank them for their kindness. That was one of the things she loved about living in the country…neighbors were always there for you, and it was a reciprocal thing. They watched out for each other.

When he carried her into the house, Claire wondered about the turkey she had left out. Jamie looked in the fridge, and wrinkled up his nose. It was well past using, and he told her he would throw it out along the road for the critters. The coyotes would make short work of it, despite the smell. She mourned the loss of the grand meal she had planned, and could almost taste the roast turkey with stuffing, as well as the cranberries and sweet potato pie she made so well. It was funny, though, how the little things didn't seem to matter now. She was alive; Mom was doing better, Jamie was here with here, and life was good. She couldn't, and wouldn't, ask for more.

Jamie went out to the truck and brought in the wheel chair, leaving it to warm up before he set her in it. He went into the kitchen, found the coffee and made a fresh pot, asking her if she was hungry. There were fixings for pancakes and her mouth watered. It sure beat the hospital food, although never once was she ungrateful for each bite she was able to eat on her own. She didn't think she would ever take food and shelter, warmth and safety for granted.

They ate at the kitchen table, pancakes dripping with sweet maple syrup and melted butter. Neither had ever enjoyed a meal as much as the simple food in front of them, shared with someone they loved. Oh, yes, she thought, I love him. All the tears, all the loneliness, all the nights spent wondering why she was alone, were just stepping stones that led her to the place she now knew she belonged…with Jamie. She looked across at him, at the strong but gentle hands, the humble man with so much love to give, and she wished he didn't have to return to Texas. Oh, she would manage around the house on her own alright, but it just wouldn't be the same without him.

As though reading her mind, he looked up and met her eyes, smiling. He reached out and gently took her hand. Her fingers had been saved, and even though the hands were still stiff and sore, they would return to normal in time. He squeezed one softly, and looked into the face that he wanted spend the rest of his life looking at when he awoke every morning. He wanted to watch her age, watch the new wisdom and awareness in her eyes, watch her brown, unruly hair start to turn silver. God, he loved this amazing creature sitting across the table from him.

"When we get done eating, I'll do up the dishes. I want you to go pack enough clothes and necessary things for a couple of weeks. The Gilberts have agreed to take care of your animals, and Frank said he would drive by occasionally to check on the house. Christmas is just a few days off, and you are coming home with me." Jamie watched her face for any sign of argument, but he didn't expect any. He got none, just a smile that lit up the whole room. His heart leaped, and he felt warm all the way to his toes.

"We have to stop by and see Mom," she said, her face growing thoughtful.

"Already planned, my dear," he laughed. "Time for me to ask her something, anyway."

Claire looked at him quizzically, but he just turned away, hands full of breakfast dishes, hiding a huge smile. She did as he asked, and wheeled her way into her bedroom. She went through her drawers and closet, taking what she thought she would need and filling a suitcase. Then she rode into the bathroom to fill a small overnight case with the usual toiletries she would use. She seldom wore makeup, so the didn't pack any, but grabbed a small bottle of her favorite perfume, which she hadn't had reason to wear in quite a while. She hoped Jamie would like the smell of it, light yet fresh and outdoorsy.

Jamie carried her back to the barn, for a last word to the animals she wouldn't see for a couple of weeks. She wasn't worried about them, though, knowing the Gilberts would take excellent care of the them, as they did their own.

Then Jamie set her in the truck, turning on the heat, and went back for the wheel chair. Remembering what she had been through, he brought out a warm woolen blanket for her peace of mind. He also grabbed two red roses from one of the gift vases she had received in the hospital. He handed her one as he got into the driver's seat, and set the other on the dashboard. Claire had the feeling her mother was about to receive a flower. She said nothing, just smiled. Oh, yeah, this was the one. The one she had dreamed of, longed for on those many nights when she wondered if love would ever come her way.

The nursing home greeted them with lots of smiles, and went with them to her mother's room. Jamie handed her mother the rose and kissed her cheek and hugged her. Her mother's arms went around him in a fond embrace, and Claire felt tears welling up in her eyes. The she noticed a suitcase next to her mother's chair, and that her mother was dressed to go out, warm coat laying across her lap. She frowned, not understanding.

"It wouldn't be right to leave your Mom alone over Christmas," he said, grinning. "So, she is coming with us. My folks can hardly wait to meet you both."

Claire let her tears fall without embarrassment, not knowing how she had gotten so lucky as to have this all happen for her. Her luck had run so bad for so long, she didn't understand how it could all turn around in a complete one hundred and eighty. Her heart swelled up so much she was afraid it would burst. A Christmas miracle had happened for her, and she silently thanked God for everything she had.

The drive down was pleasant and comfortable, and her mother seemed lucid and excited to be going on an adventure. Jamie was a good man, and she was so pleased that Claire had had the good sense to get away from that selfish rascal, David. Claire would have a good life with this young man, and she knew that they were perfect for each other. They were the old-fashioned kind of young people, the kind that believed in working hard, pulling together in harness, and fixing what went wrong instead of throwing in the towel.

Jamie's folks weren't the pretentious sort, totally comfortable with a modest, two-story brick and siding house. The yard was well kept, and it was obvious that during the warmer months, the gardens were full of flowers. The front paddocks were all fenced in white board, and the stables and barns were painted and clean. It was a ranch that someone loved and took pride in keeping up.

Christmas lights were already hung, strands of red and green and blue, gracing the house and front fence as well as the Norway pines out front of the house. Large plastic candy canes lined the driveway with garlands of green pine boughs interlocking them. It seemed there were lights everywhere! How festive it looked, and how Claire and mother loved to see an appreciation of the season they had missed so much since Dad had passed away. They exchanged glances, both smiling from ear to ear.

A dark red, glossy-coated dog ran out to the truck, barking and wagging it's whole hind end. A man came out of the stables, and waved, a huge smile on his face. A woman with a white apron stepped out from the front door, a matching smile on her face. Not only was their son home, but he had brought his lady with him, along with her mother. What a wonderful way it was to get to know them both, but what a delightful Christmas it would be! Family, friends, enough to eat, and blessings of all kinds abounding. A home should be filled with people on Christmas, and noise and laughter and good times. All of the kids would be here this year, along with the sweet and rowdy grand children.

They all converged on the truck, introductions were made, and as Jamie lifted Claire out of the vehicle and set her in the chair, his father took Claire's mother gently by the arm and led her to the house. There was even a temporary ramp built for Claire's wheel chair. They all followed, met by warmth and hospitality, and the dog was allowed to come in, is well. Claire noticed, and was gratified, that they treated the dog as part of the family. A dog's owners were that animal's family, their pack, and it was together that they belonged, as far as Claire was concerned.

Claire and her mother would be sharing a room, so that Claire could keep an eye on her during those times when Mom forgot where she was, or what she was doing. There were two twin beds, covered in bright, soft patchwork quilts in peach and emerald, and soft, fluffy rugs of sea foam green . The Pricilla curtains were pulled back with flowered ties, giving them a wonderful view of the paddocks behind the barn. Horses grazed contentedly, swishing their tails and moving a few steps on when the choice bits of grass were gone.

Claire helped her mother unpack, and then used the second, smaller dresser for herself. What a grand Christmas this would be! Not only did she and her mother NOT have to spend it in the elderly care facility, but they would be enjoying the company of new friends in a warm, holiday-decorated home and eating a huge meal with children, which was a new experience for Claire. She had never heard the excited chatter of small voices, or the sound of little feet running around in high spirits. Her heart swelled as she looked at her mother, so beautiful even in her later years. Her hair was silver, accentuating her blue-gray eyes, and her face has more color than usual, blushed by the excitement. Claire was so proud of her, for weathering the storms she had endured, for retaining a sweet nature, never complaining.

Mom had brought her fiddle with her, hoping to play Christmas music for whoever would listen. She drew it out of it's case, tightened her bow and rosined it, and drew it across the strings to make sure they were still in tune. She could hear a hymn from the den's stereo, and played along. Claire sat enthralled, as she always was when Mom played. She never missed a note, a beat, and made that old fiddle sing like an angel.

Jamie's mother stood at the door, meaning to ask if they needed anything, but when she heard the music in Claire's room, she stood spellbound, listening. She moved away quietly, and went to get her husband. They both stood in the doorway, enjoying the skill and love that came from the woman's hands. His mother held something behind her back, then brought forth her own violin.

"May I join you?" she requested, eyes shining. Claire's mother nodded, a big smile on her aging face. They had something in common! This would be a special visit, indeed! The two woman sat across from each other, and played their hearts out; one played the melody, one played the harmony. One song after another, they joined in friendship that would bloom for years to come. Jamie's dad threw a comforting arm around Claire and she smiled up at him, eyes brimming.

Claire had the chance to help in the kitchen, making her feel useful, and giving her a chance to get to know them all better. Even from the wheelchair, she was able to make pies and cakes and cookies that would tickle the taste buds of everyone on Christmas day. She could hear the to women playing music, and heard Jamie and his father talking about the weather, the price of hay, the condition of the cattle and how nice it would be if Jamie were to consider coming home after his tour was up. Although Jamie's oldest brother came out to help on the ranch every day after work, it did take away time from his own wife and children, and left him little time for rest and relaxation. Jamie had been thinking of it, himself, and told his father that it was a distinct possibility. He DID miss the life on the ranch.

Claire heard the back door open, the third morning that they were there, and Jamie came to get her from the kitchen.

"I have someone I want you to meet," he laughed. Wheeling her into the den, she was attacked by a litter of Irish Setter puppies, twelve weeks old, and ready to lick her to death. There were five of them, three of them already promised to good homes. The two left were as different from day and night. The little male was rowdy and gregarious, bouncing around the house like his legs were spring-loaded. The larger female was a bit shy, content to sit and watch the shenanigans of her siblings. She wasn't as bright red as the other pups, her coat being a duller auburn, almost dusty red. She looked at Claire and walked up to her, sniffing the offered hand, then licked it softly. Claire gathered her up into her arms and she settled on Claire's lap contentedly. The little animal was warm and enjoyed being the center of someone's attention. That was all Jamie needed to see. He walked out of the room and left the animals with Claire.

On December 23, the rest of Jamie's family began to arrive, and the house started to fill up. It was a riot of hugs and introductions, laughter and catching up on the past. Jamie's brother Michael showed up with his wife, Donna, and their two children, Shawn and Brandy. Then Tyrrell and Gwinn came in, with Amber and Alicia. The house was constantly in motion, and the pups added chaos to the mixture. Claire wondered how her mother would handle the ruckus, until she saw that Amber showed an avid interest in Mom's fiddle, and the older woman was more than pleased to show her how to hold it and draw the bow across the strings. Brandy stuck close to Claire, wanting to help with the baking of the dozens of cookies that wouldn't see December 26th. Claire enjoyed the commotion, wondering what it would be like to have children of her own.

Presents in colorful wrappings and bows began to fill the space beneath the Christmas tree, mountains of boxes and packages that the puppies had to be chased away from. The fireplace burned constantly, filling the room with the scent of oak to mingle with the aromas of pine, cinnamon, and baking. Music added flavor, and laughter spilled out of every room. Claire couldn't imagine a finer get-together. She had missed the love and companionship found during the holidays, and she found herself weeping often at the beauty of family times.

Christmas Eve morning dawned fair and decidedly warm for December in Texas. Birds sang and flew about, the foals were playing in the sunshine, kicking up their little heels, and the children got to play outside, leaving the adults a little peace and quiet. The puppies were outside with them, and Claire sat back in her chair, enjoying her first cup of coffee with Jamie at the table. She glance at the eight foot tree in the living room, almost hidden by presents. She felt bad about not having anything to give, and voiced her sadness to Jamie.

"Aw, Honey, you were kind of busy trying to stay alive, you know," Jamie answered. "It's not like you knew you were coming down here and had time to go shopping. Besides, your mother and you being here is a wonderful gift, to all of us."

"You always know how to make someone feel better," Claire smiled. "I still wish I had something for everyone."

"You do, you just don't know it yet." Jamie rose to refill their mugs with hot coffee.

Her mother came in, dressed warmly in wool slacks and a warm fluffy sweater. She got a cup from the cupboard and joined them at the large honey colored oak table. She sipped the aromatic brew in silence for a few minutes, then turned to Jamie with a soft smile.

"I want to thank you personally for bringing us down here to spend Christmas with you and your family. Holidays have been rather lonely for Claire since I went to live at the home. Yes, she spends them with me, but I know I am not always in my right mind and it is hard for her. This is wonderful, being around such warm and generous folks."

"You have added to the spirit of the season," Jamie smiled. "Your music is such a gift, and I know my mom is tickled to have someone to play it with."

"I haven't heard you play so much in a very long time, Mom," Claire sighed contentedly. "I have so missed that."

"Me, too, Honey. Me, too. Now, I think I will go out and play along with the children. I hear a Nerf ball calling my name." And out the back door she went, to the shouted greetings of the children.

Christmas Eve dinner consisted of homegrown steaks, baked potatoes, and green beans, picked at the peak of their season and frozen to enjoy when the growing season was long over. Desert was a red velvet cake that Claire had baked and topped with sweet cream cheese frosting. It was a big hit, and all of the other women asked her for her recipe. She was delighted to share it, and made her feel as though she had at least contributed something. No one left the table until they were so full that they were groaning and laughing, after which they all retired to the den with coffee. It was the custom to open one gift on Christmas Eve, leaving the remaining gifts for the morning. The children were all old enough to know that there was no Santa Clause, just their parents and relatives giving them gifts they had wished for.

The children tore open wrappings, dancing with excitement as they revealed small gifts that pleased them immensely. Shawn got the first National Geographic magazine of a two year subscription. Brandy opened a small package and squealed with delight as she held up the moonstone and silver necklace she had seen in a catalog and bugged her grandmother for for months. Alicia got a book of birds, so she could more easily identify the backyard birds she loved to feed. Amber received the musical unicorn statue she had asked for. It played 'Camelot', and she wound it up time and again. There was a beautiful scarf of cashmere for Jamie's mother, and three pair of wool socks for his father. Everyone opened up a gift, including Claire's mother, who found a new set of strings for her fiddle.

Jamie handed Claire a small package, wrapped in blue and silver paper with a dainty silver bow. She fumbled with the paper covering, and looked at him love in her eyes. Inside the wrapping was a small oblong box, tied with silver string. When she untied it and opened the box, there was a silver, heart-shaped locket that would hold a picture on each half of the heart. On the left side was the small photo of her mother and father that Jamie had searched so hard for. The right side was empty, waiting to hold a picture of Claire's choice. She felt her heart swell, and her eyes brimmed with tears.

"All I have to give you is my heart," she whispered.

"That is all I wanted," Jamie told her, finally getting the first kiss he had longed for. "It's all I needed."

The whole family watched as love bloomed before their eyes, and smiles lit up all around the room, except for the children, who thought the whole love thing was just gross. Shawn rolled is eyes, Brandy stuck her finger in her throat in mock gagging, and the two younger girls just giggled. It had been a perfect evening.

Christmas morning came with a dusting of snow. Red cardinals and blue jays perched on the bird feeder, and the puppies rolled about in the snow they had never experienced before. The horses were up by the fence, munching on the flakes of hay thrown to them, and the cattle were laying in the hollow behind the big barn.

Breakfast would wait, as was the custom here, until all gifts had been opened. Shouts of happiness and laughter filled the room, and mounds of torn wrapping paper were piling up on the floor. When the last gift was opened and admired and hugs and thank yous had quieted down, Jamie stood up, looking around in confusion. He tossed wrapping paper aside, making a bigger mess, then looked behind the tree, behind the sofa, and under a chair. It looked as though he had lost a present in the confusion. Then he straightened up, snapped his fingers, and his face lit up. He hurried from the room, leaving everyone looking at him as though he were crazy.

He came back in a few moments later, carrying a huge box, wrapped in the blue and silver paper he had chosen just for Claire. He set it down on the floor in front of Claire's wheel chair, and stood back, arms crossed over his chest.

"One more," he grinned. "I almost forgot it."

The bow quivered strangely, and Claire gave him a raised eyebrow, but smiled. Bending over to lift the lid, the female pup popped her head up and barked. Everyone laughed, except for Claire. The little dog wasn't the only thing in the big box. Claire bent again and pulled up a twenty pound bag of kibble, and taped to the bag was a flea collar much too big for the small pup. Attached to the collar was a set of tags, and when she fingered them to see them closer, it turned out to be Jamie's dog tags.

"I don't know how to chase 'possums," he laughed, "But I'm willing to learn."

- The End -